The Wat

Written by Jo Windsor

Rigby

The lion is
at the water hole.

The baby lion is
at the water hole, too.

The elephant is
at the water hole.

The baby elephant is at the water hole, too.

The giraffe is
at the water hole.

The baby giraffe is
at the water hole, too.

Index

animals at
the water hole

Guide Notes

Title: The Water Hole

Stage: Emergent – Magenta

Genre: Nonfiction (Expository)

Approach: Guided Reading

Processes: Thinking Critically, Exploring Language, Processing Information

Written and Visual Focus: Photographs (static images), Index

Word Count: 48

FORMING THE FOUNDATION

Tell the children that this book is about different animals that come to the water hole.
Talk to them about what is on the front cover. Read the title and the author.
Focus the children's attention on the index and talk about the different animals that are in this book.
"Walk" through the book, focusing on the photographs and talk about the animals and their babies and what they are doing.

Read the text together.

THINKING CRITICALLY
(sample questions)

After the reading
• What do you think would happen if the animals did not have a water hole?
• What is different about the way the lion and the elephant get the water?

EXPLORING LANGUAGE
(ideas for selection)

Terminology
Title, cover, author, photographs

Vocabulary
Interest words: lion, baby, elephant, giraffe
High-frequency words: the, is, at, the